.m. GRAND STATION ✵MYSTERY TOUR✵

THE MYSTERY EXPRESS

illustrated by Pam Adams

Child's Play (International) Ltd
© 1983 M. Twinn   ISBN 0-85953-180-5   Printed in Singapore

Early in the morning,
the train leaves the station
and rumbles through the town

TO WOODLAND HALT

. . . into the countryside.
Do the cows know
where we are going?

WOODLAND
HALT

Our first stop is in the wood.
Is there time for a picnic?

TO THE LAND OF FANTASY

We cross the wide river.

Next stop is Fairy Glen.
Now there is magic on board!

DANGER
DEAD SLOW
Rabbits and moles at work!

I hope we don't stay
underground for long!

Giants live in the mountains.

BIG DIPPER

Ride of a lifetime

whee!

◄TICKETS

THE GHOST TRAIN

TICKETS►

SPOOKY JUNCTION

Last stop before the beach